A DREIDEL IN TIME

A NEW SPIN ON AN OLD TALE

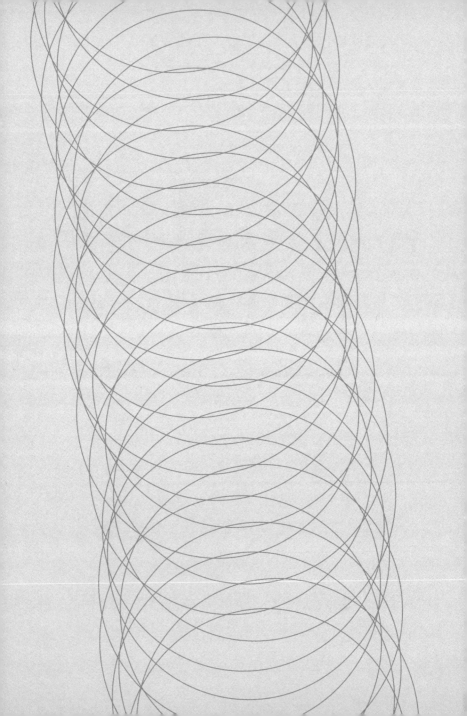

A DREIDEL IN TIME

A NEW SPIN ON AN OLD TALE

MARCIA BERNEGER

ILLUSTRATED BY BEATRIZ CASTRO

KAR-BEN
PUBLISHING

This book is dedicated to Eric—
my lifelong partner and co-conspirator on our
adventurous journey through life.

Text copyright © 2019 by Marcia Berneger
Illustrations copyright © 2019 by Lerner Publishing Group, Inc.

KAR-BEN PUBLISHING, INC.
An imprint of Lerner Publishing Group, Inc.
241 First Avenue North
Minneapolis, MN 55401 USA
1-800-4-KARBEN

Website address: www.karben.com

Main body text set in Bembo Std regular 12.5/17.
Typeface provided by Monotype Typography.

Library of Congress Cataloging-in-Publication Data

Names: Berneger, Marcia, 1952– author.
Title: A dreidel in time : a new spin on an old tale / Marcia Berneger.
Description: Minneapolis, MN : Kar-Ben Publishing, [2019] | Summary:
    A brother and sister receive a strange Hanukkah gift and family
    heirloom—a magic dreidel that take them back in time to learn about the
    true meaning of Hanukkah.
Identifiers: LCCN 2018035865| ISBN 9781541546721 (lb : alk. paper) |
    ISBN 9781541552654 (pb : alk. paper)
Subjects: | CYAC: Hanukkah—Fiction. | Maccabees—Fiction. | Jews—
    History—586 B.C.-70 A.D.—Fiction. | Time travel—Fiction. | Brothers
    and sisters—Fiction.
Classification: LCC PZ7.1.B46 Dr 2019 | DDC [Fic]—dc23

LC record available at https://lccn.loc.gov/2018035865

Manufactured in the United States of America
2 - 48386 - 41663 - 10/21/2019

TABLE OF CONTENTS

CHAPTER 1
HANUKKAH

"PSST . . . Benjamin!"

Benjamin looked up from the kitchen table. His sister, Devorah, was wiggling her finger at him to join her at the closet under their staircase. "Is that where you think Mom hid our Hanukkah presents this time?" he asked. "Don't bother . . . I've already looked there."

Devorah walked over to the table. "So, smarty pants, where do you think they are?"

"She's probably got them someplace we can't get to, like her car trunk. She got pretty mad at us last year, remember?"

"That's because when we found them, you opened yours."

"I was only eight years old!" Benjamin picked up

his pencil. "I've got to finish my math homework before Mom comes home from work, or she won't let me open any presents tonight. She and Dad will be home any minute."

"Mom said they might be late because they have to pick up some sour cream for the latkes." Devorah looked at the hanukkiah set up on the dining room table. Eight candles stood in a row, led by the shamash, a candle raised above the others. It always reminded Devorah of a general leading his army into a battle against darkness. "We can help Mom by lighting the candles."

Benjamin's wrinkled his eyebrows. "We'd better wait for her to get home."

"I'm having my Bat Mitzvah next year. I'm old enough to handle the lighter."

"That's not what I meant. She's already complaining about how the only thing we think about on Hanukkah is opening our presents."

"Come on. Say the blessings with me. She won't be as mad if we tell her we lit them together."

"Maybe." Benjamin joined her as she lit the shamash. She plucked it out of its holder and lit the other candles.

The front door opened just as Devorah lit the

eighth candle. She replaced the shamash in its holder, then ran over and gave Mom a big hug. "Hi. Let me take your coat and hang it up for you. How was your day?"

"I bet you're hungry," Benjamin chimed in. "I'm starving. Can we make the potato latkes now?"

"You're starving?" Mom chuckled. "I didn't think we were *that* late." She handed Devorah her coat and glanced at the clock on the kitchen wall. "It's only 5:00. I'd like to rest a bit before starting the latkes. If you want to speed things up, you can peel the potatoes."

Benjamin returned to the table and opened his math book. "Devorah only wants to eat so she can open tonight's Hanukkah present. That's why she lit the candles before you got home."

Devorah glared at her brother.

Mom frowned. "You lit the candles without us?"

"You were late and it got dark." Devorah grinned. "Benjamin didn't think you'd mind."

"Don't you shove that off on me!" Benjamin looked at his sister. "Lighting the candles was your idea!"

Dad shook his head. "I suppose if you knew where your presents were hidden, you'd have opened them already, too!"

Devorah's face reddened as she and her brother exchanged glances.

"Speaking of presents . . ." Benjamin smiled.

Mom sighed. "Well, tonight you'll have to wait even longer. Your grandparents are joining us for dinner. They'll be here in a half hour or so." Mom sank into her comfy chair.

"Bubbe and Zayde are coming! Hooray!" cried Benjamin. "I sure hope they bring me the art set I asked for."

"And the telescope I want!" added Devorah.

"Bubbe is bringing you both a very special gift this year."

"What is it?" Devorah and Benjamin shouted at the same time.

"You'll have to wait and see." Mom closed her eyes. "But I guarantee you—it will be, to use your words, 'awesome.'"

CHAPTER 2
THE GIFT

When their grandparents arrived, there were lots of hugs from Zayde and smushes into Bubbe's soft, round tummy.

"We're so glad you're here!" said Benjamin. "I have a Hanukkah present for you. I painted it myself. I can give it to you now, if you want."

"What a great idea! Let's exchange our gifts now." Devorah walked over to her grandmother.

Zayde patted the couch. "Buzz on over here, my little bumblebee."

Devorah snuggled next to him. She liked when he called her that, since her name, Devorah, meant "bee" in Hebrew.

"Just this once, how would you like your gift before dinner?"

Benjamin came over. "Really, Zayde? We can open our presents now?"

Bubbe brought in an elegantly wrapped box. "One present to share," she said.

Devorah's smile disappeared. The box was too small and too light to be a telescope. And a gift to share with her brother didn't sound like fun at all. She took the box from Bubbe and held it for a long time.

"*Nu*, so open it already and find out what's inside," said Zayde.

Devorah slid the ribbon off the box, opened it, and took out a large, bubble-wrapped object.

"What is it?" Benjamin asked.

Devorah peeled off the bubble wrap.

Benjamin wrinkled up his face. "What is this?"

"It's a dreidel," said Bubbe. "Didn't you learn to play the dreidel game in your Sunday school?"

"I've seen lots of dreidels," said Devorah. "And none of them have looked anything like this one." She turned it over in her hands. For one thing, it was large for a dreidel. And it was lopsided, and speckled red and gray with fancy Hebrew letters.

Devorah's disappointment kept her from thanking her grandparents as she knew she should. "This has got to be the strangest dreidel I have ever seen. I'm sorry, Bubbe, I don't mean to be rude, and it's probably an old dreidel and special to you, but it sure is . . . not very pretty."

"It doesn't have to be pretty to work," Zayde told her. "Why don't you sit on the floor together and give it a spin?"

"You mean, you gave us a dreidel so we can play the game together? Like a family-time thing?" Benjamin laughed. "I have a dreidel that will work much better than this one." He stood up. "Do you want me to get it?"

Mom shook her head. "Let's try this one. When your Uncle Robert and I were young, we were just like you, always in a hurry to get to the Hanukkah gifts. But then one night Bubbe insisted we get into the *real* spirit of Hanukkah. It's not just about gifts. She took out this very same old dreidel. And as we played, the real meaning of Hanukkah surrounded us and . . ."

"O-oh, I get it," said Benjamin. "*You* played with this dreidel when you were our age. Now it's *our* turn to carry on that tradition." He plopped down on the floor. "Okay. Let's do this."

"But after we play the game, we can open our real presents, right?" Devorah joined her brother on the floor. She turned the dreidel slowly between her fingers, looking at the four Hebrew letters, one on each side. They had just played the game in Sunday school. Each player had put a chocolate coin in the center of the table. When you spun the dreidel, the letter it landed on told you whether you'd won or lost your coins.

"Where are the chocolate coins?" Benjamin licked his lips.

Bubbe's eyes twinkled. "You won't need chocolate coins with this dreidel. It's magic. Spin it and you'll see what I mean."

Neither child noticed the grown-ups fade away as Devorah gave the funny-looking driedel a spin. "I barely spun it," she whispered to her brother, "so it should drop quickly."

But instead of slowing, the top sped up.

"What's happening?" Benjamin cried. The dreidel spun faster and faster until the whole room whirled with it. He grabbed onto Devorah and shut his eyes.

And then it stopped, just like that!

Devorah shook her brother's arm. "Benjamin, look!"

Benjamin opened one eye. The dreidel had

fallen on its side. A Hebrew letter glowed on its upper face.

Devorah trembled as she stared at the letter.

A *Shin* . . . a bad spin. In the dreidel game, it meant you lost something.

CHAPTER 3
SHIN

The children looked up from the dreidel. Their living room had disappeared, replaced by a raggedy old tent. "Where *are* we?" Devorah whispered.

"That crazy dreidel must have put me to sleep," Benjamin said, more to himself than out loud. "This is one bad dream!"

"Well, if it's a dream, I'm having the same one as you!" Devorah touched the furry animal skin they were sitting on. "Maybe if we spin the dreidel again, we'll wake up." She reached for the dreidel. It vanished right before her eyes.

"Oh, no!" they both cried.

"This dream is pretty weird!" Benjamin got up and turned around. "Look at my baggy pants and shirt."

Devorah stood up, too. She was wearing a white linen dress. She dusted herself off and sneezed.

"*Gesundheit!*" said her brother. "I bet if we go outside, we'll wake up and be back home in our living room."

He headed toward the tent flap. Devorah grabbed his arm. "Benjamin, I don't think we're dreaming."

"What do you mean? Of course we are." He tried to shake free. "Or else it's some kind of trick to teach us a lesson. Bubbe and Zayde are probably standing right outside this tent."

"You stay here. I'll check." Devorah let go of her brother's arm and walked to the tent flaps. Her hand shook as she parted the flaps slightly. Slowly, she peeked through the small crack. "Oh, my!" she said with a gasp.

"Wh-what's out there?" asked her brother.

"Benjamin, we're not in Los Angeles any more."

He tiptoed to her side and looked out. "No way! Maybe the dreidel somehow brought us to a movie set in Hollywood?"

Devorah shook her head. "Those stone and clay buildings look real. So does the dirt road, and this tent we're in. Everything seems old. I mean really old, like hundreds—no, thousands!—of years old."

"That's crazy!" shouted Benjamin. "How can that be?"

"Look—there's a Jewish building . . . a small temple, maybe." Devorah pointed to a building with a large Star of David carved above the doorway. "The dreidel must have brought us to a Jewish town from long ago."

A crowd of townspeople, all dressed in linen, were gathered in front of the temple. A group of soldiers stood nearby. An man in a long, white robe pushed through the crowd. Even though he was very old, the people all turned to hear his words.

"We have had enough of your laws." He shook his wooden staff at the soldiers. "These are not our laws and we will no longer obey them!"

Benjamin turned to his sister. "His words sound funny."

"I recognize that language from Sunday school. He's speaking Hebrew," explained Devorah.

Benjamin listened carefully to what the old man was saying. "Yeah, you're right. But how come I understand him? I don't speak Hebrew."

"Me neither, at least not that well. But I understand him, too." She put her finger to her lips. "Shh! I want to hear what he's saying."

The old man's piercing eyes searched the crowd. "You there, Ruben." Everyone backed away from Ruben, who was holding a squealing pig and a long, sharp knife.

The old man straightened his back and spoke to Ruben. "We are Jews. We will not sacrifice to the king's gods. Release the pig!"

Ruben refused. "The king has ordered us to sacrifice a pig, Mattisyahu. One of us must obey these soldiers or we will all suffer. I will be that someone!"

The old man marched up to Ruben, raised his staff, and struck him. The young man crumpled to the ground. A murmur drifted through the crowd. A few heads turned toward the soldiers. The king's guards were pointing at the fallen man and laughing. Then they turned and walked away.

The old man addressed the townspeople. "We will not do as the Syrian king demands. If you agree with me, then join me. We will leave here and be free to follow our Jewish laws." He turned and touched the shoulder of a nearby man. "Come, my son. Gather your family and what possessions you can carry. We must leave Modi'in immediately."

The crowd hurried to their homes. Everyone returned carrying bundles of clothing and food.

Benjamin looked at Devorah. "What's going on? What should we do?"

"I don't know, but it's not safe here. The soldiers will get angry when everyone leaves. Since we're dressed like the townspeople, we'd better go too. We need to find someone who can help us figure this out." Devorah pointed to two children trailing behind the group. "This way," she said, grabbing her brother's hand. They raced toward the departing townspeople.

CHAPTER 4
SIMON AND SHOSHANA

"We need to stay close to those kids," Devorah whispered to Benjamin. He just stared at her.

"What? Do you think we should do something else?" she asked.

He shook his head. "No . . . It's . . . you're speaking Hebrew!"

"But you can understand me, right?"

Her brother nodded.

"Listen to yourself. You're speaking Hebrew too. This must be part of the dreidel's magic." Devorah slowed as they caught up to a tall, skinny boy. "Why is everyone leaving?" she asked, panting.

The boy glared at her. "I haven't seen you before. Where are you from?" he demanded.

"I'm Devorah and this is my brother, Benjamin.

We just arrived. There were so many soldiers in your town, we got scared. We were afraid to stay in the town when we saw everyone leaving."

The boy eyed her suspiciously. "What town are you from?"

Devorah tried to remember what the old man had said. Which city did he name? Should she name a city in Israel—if that's even where they were?

"We're from Jerusalem," said Benjamin.

Devorah looked at him, then at the boy. Jerusalem must have worked. At least the boy had stopped glaring at them.

"I am Shoshana and this is my brother, Simon," said the girl. "Where are your parents? Shouldn't they be traveling with you?"

"You're here without your parents, aren't you?" Benjamin said. Shoshana didn't answer but her eyes filled with tears. She hurried to catch up to her brother.

"Why are you all running away from your homes?" Devorah asked Simon.

"We have to leave Modi'in because of the soldiers."

Modi'in. That was what the old man had said. *That town sounds familiar,* thought Devorah.

"We have always had kings ruling over us. But this new one, this Antiochus . . ." Simon spat out the name. "He is evil."

Devorah caught her breath. Antiochus? It couldn't be. She glanced at her brother. His eyebrows were once again scrunched together. Was he thinking the same thing? Modi'in was the ancient town in the Hanukkah story. And Antiochus was the king who ruled over the town. Devorah remembered that, in the Hanukkah story, he'd made life so unbearable the townspeople had fled to the hills.

"Antiochus has ordered his soldiers to kill anyone they find observing Jewish traditions," added Shoshana. "That's why Mattisyahu is leading us away. We want to practice our religion in peace."

Simon continued. "My father was teaching me about the Torah." Simon paused, his voice catching in his throat. "The soldiers found out. They took him and our mother away this past summer, two days before my thirteenth birthday."

"I was in the field with Simon. We were gathering flowers to surprise our mother for the Sabbath. If we had been home, we would have been taken as well."

Simon put his arm around his sister and they walked together in silence.

Benjamin pulled his sister to the side. "What are we going to do?"

"Shh." Devorah took her brother's hand. "We can't do anything right now."

"But how will we get back home?" Benjamin whispered.

"I don't know, but that dreidel somehow brought us here. If we can find it, maybe it will take us home."

CHAPTER 5
CAMP

The group stopped in a clearing somewhere in the dry, dusty hills above Modi'in. A large tent had been set up. Small campsites were spread out around it.

"Over here!" Simon called out. "This is a good spot for us."

Shoshana joined her brother. They removed the thorny sagebrush and stones from a small area.

Devorah pulled her brother aside. "Let's clear our own spot near theirs," she whispered, pushing a large tumbleweed out of the area. "Hey, come and help me."

But Benjamin plopped down where he was. "I'm tired. We've walked all day."

"You can rest when we're done. The sun is setting and it'll be dark soon." She tugged on her brother's arm. "Unless you're so tired, the rocks and thorns won't bother you tonight."

Benjamin frowned as he got up. He kicked away the small rocks. "Ow!" he cried, kicking a rock that was stuck in the hard ground. "This is crazy!"

Shoshana came over to him. "My brother and I have finished clearing our area. I can help you for a little while."

"Thanks," said Benjamin. He looked around. "I'm hungry and I'm tired. I want to go home!" he blinked, trying not to cry.

"I know you're afraid. I am too. Maybe we can help each other until . . . until our parents all return." Shoshana moved away some of the sagebrush.

Benjamin got up and they worked together until the area was smooth. Devorah smiled as she watched them. She was glad they had found Shoshana and Simon.

The sun set, and the campsite was covered in darkness. The only light came from the large fire blazing in the center of the camp.

The Maccabees and their families straggled over to the fire.

"You'd better stay with us," Simon told them. "People are worried about the soldiers following us . . . and about spies. Some have already noticed you. They are wondering why you are here with us . . . as am I."

Shoshana stood. "Don't worry. We'll bring you some food and something to drink. But my brother's right. You should stay here. You'll be safer for now."

Devorah and Benjamin sat on the bits of grass they had found to soften the ground. Their new friends returned. Shoshana handed them some dried cheese and fruit, two pieces of flat bread, and a small flask of water. It wasn't much, but it stopped the rumbling in their stomachs. Simon tossed them each a blanket.

Benjamin and Devorah spread out the blankets. "These are really scratchy," whispered Benjamin. "And the ground is too hard. I'll never get to sleep."

"Just be thankful Simon found these blankets for us, or you'd be cold as well," said Devorah.

Benjamin rolled toward his sister. "Devorah, what's going on?"

"Bubbe's dreidel must have brought us back to the time when Hanukkah first started. These are the real people from Modi'in. Those men we saw must be Mattisyahu, his son Judah, and the Jewish Maccabee soldiers!"

"But everything is terrible here." Benjamin's voice shook. "The people had to leave their homes to live . . . here! And Simon and Shoshana—their parents are gone. Maybe even dead. This isn't anything like the story they told us in Sunday school!"

"Oh, no!" Devorah sat up. "The story— remember what happens? Antiochus sends his soldiers after the Maccabees. They'll have to fight his soldiers here in the hills. The Maccabees have to prepare for the battle."

"You're right. We've got to warn Simon!"

Devorah nodded. "I saw him head toward the campfire a few minutes ago."

The children crept toward the blazing campfire. They had not gone far when two men grabbed them.

"Who are you?" A large man shook Benjamin. "Tell me, boy!"

"This one," said his partner, shaking his head, "is a girl. We should take them to Mattisyahu. He will know how to deal with spies!"

CHAPTER 6
THE WARNING

The men dragged the frightened children to the campfire. They were shoved in front of the old man.

"Jonathan and I found these two spies, Father," said Benjamin's captor.

Devorah looked up at Mattisyahu, tears in her eyes. "We were trying to find Simon to warn him, to warn all of you," she whispered.

Mattisyahu's glare softened as he looked at her. "To warn us of what, child?"

Benjamin rubbed his bruised arms. "To warn you that Antiochus plans to send his soldiers to kill you!"

Mattisyahu studied Benjamin for a long moment. Then he motioned to the man holding

Benjamin. "You may release him, Judah."

Judah shoved Benjamin forward.

"Come here, boy." Mattisyahu smiled. "Tell me who you are and why you have journeyed here with us."

"I'm Benjamin, and this is my sister, Devorah. We come from . . . from Jerusalem." He looked over at his sister.

Devorah continued. "Antiochus' soldiers took our parents away. We were afraid they would come back for us."

"We saw you heading away from Modi'in," added her brother, "and decided we'd better join you because . . ."

"Because we knew we'd be safer hiding with you. If the soldiers were after you, they'd be after us, too," finished Devorah. "And they *are* after you, or they will be soon. You have to get ready to fight them!"

Mattisyahu took Devorah's hands into his own strong grasp. "Child," he said. "To Antiochus we are like a small band of insects. He will not bother with us. Stay here; you will be safe."

"You don't know Antiochus," snapped Benjamin. "He will come after you!"

"Don't be fooled, Father." Judah placed his hand on his sword. "These children are sure the soldiers will fight us because they are spies. How else would they know these plans?"

"If we're spies," argued Benjamin, "then why are we warning you?"

"You say we'll be safe here, but when the soldiers come, no one will be safe!" Devorah looked into the old man's face.

"Please, send someone to check." Benjamin softened his voice. "I'm so scared."

"You would like us to do that, wouldn't you?" Judah turned to face Mattisyahu. "We'd be walking into a trap!"

Mattisyahu sighed. "Take Jonathan and return to Modi'in. Search the area, determine the soldiers' plans, then report back to me."

"But, Father," Judah protested, grabbing Benjamin and yanking him to his feet. "You can't let these two spies roam freely. They're sure to escape and travel back to Modi'in to warn the soldiers."

Mattisyahu's brow wrinkled. "I do not think they are much of a threat. But, there is a small cave behind the women's tent. Put them there and post a guard. We can sort out their story when you return from Modi'in." He waved Judah and Jonathan away. The two men stomped off and shoved Benjamin and Devorah into the cave.

"Ow!" grumbled Benjamin, bumping his head as Judah tossed him into the cave. "This stupid thing is so small, we can't even both lie down to sleep at the same time."

"Well, at least we warned them. Everything will be okay once Judah returns from Modi'in. He'll tell Mattisyahu about the soldiers and then they'll have to believe us."

Benjamin scrunched to the back of the tiny cave. "Ouch!" he cried again, sitting on something hard. He reached around.

"Devorah!" he shouted. "I've found Bubbe's dreidel! Now we can go home!" The children huddled together, glad to be going home. Glad to be free of this nightmare.

Benjamin held onto Devorah while she gave the dreidel a spin. The top picked up speed, faster and faster, until the whole cave swirled.

Then it stopped, just like that!

The Hebrew letter *Nun* glowed up at them.

Devorah and Benjamin stared at the dreidel. *Nun.* In the dreidel game it means nothing happens;

you neither gain nor lose.

"Devorah!" shouted Benjamin, tears filling his eyes as he glanced up. "It didn't work! Nothing's changed!"

Devorah stared out. They were still in the campsite on the dust-covered hillside. Everything was the same as before. Or was it?

נ

CHAPTER 7
NUN

"Devorah, we're not home! What happened? Why are we still here in this cave?" Benjamin searched for the dreidel, but it was gone.

The children crawled out and looked around. Something *had* changed. The camp was now well-organized, as if it had been there for a long time.

Before they could figure it out, two teens burst into view.

Devorah stared at them. They looked familiar. Suddenly Benjamin shouted, "Simon! Shoshana!"

"Devorah, Benjamin, you've returned!" cried Shoshana.

"Returned?" said Devorah. "We never left. But, you both look . . . older."

Simon spoke. "I'm fifteen now, and Shoshana is twelve. But you haven't aged at all. What magic do you possess that keeps you from aging?"

Devorah explained about the dreidel. "It's a top that spins around. There are four Hebrew letters on it. A *Shin*, a *Nun*, a *Hey*, and a *Gimmel*. They stand for 'a great miracle happened there.' You know—it's part of the holiday . . . of Hanukkah."

Simon's voice rose. "Your story is nonsense. There's no holiday called Hanukkah."

Devorah pulled her brother aside. "The Hanukkah story is happening right now. It hasn't become a holiday yet."

"Oh, yeah. You're right." Benjamin bit his lip. "How do we convince them our story is true?"

Simon looked around. "And where is this magic spinning toy of yours? Show me how it works," he demanded.

"It . . . it disappears after we spin it," Benjamin said.

Simon's eyes narrowed.

Shoshana walked over to Benjamin. "So if you find it, will it take you back to another time?"

"We don't really know," Devorah answered. "I guess the dreidel moves us through time somehow. It took us to Modi'in when you all were leaving, and it brought us here now. It's all very confusing. It's two years later for you, but only a few seconds later for us. I can't explain it."

A group of Maccabees passed them. Benjamin turned to Simon. "What's happening?" he asked. "Did the soldiers come like we said?"

"Your information was correct," Shoshana said. "Judah and Jonathan discovered the soldiers of Antiochus *were* planning to attack us. But Judah was convinced you were spies when he returned and found you both gone."

"I agree with Judah." Simon crossed his arms over his chest. "You haven't convinced me with your story of magic and this . . . dreidel . . ."

"But, Simon, they did save us from being captured by the soldiers . . . or worse."

Simon sighed. "My sister is right. Whatever you are, your warning gave us enough time to organize our army."

"So Mattisyahu and his men are winning?" asked Benjamin.

"Not Mattisyahu. He died bravely in battle. His son Judah, leads us now." Simon stood up, pushing out his chest. "I'm a soldier now. And Shoshana helps care for the injured."

"But you're not a grown-up! Why are you fighting?" Devorah asked.

"Antiochus has sent too many soldiers. Everyone who is thirteen and older has to fight. Even younger children help by serving food or cleaning up," said Shoshana.

"Our battle is critical," said Simon. "If we don't win this war, everyone will be forced to worship as the ruling king demands. We battle for the freedom to follow our traditions. We fight for the Jewish people, and for all other people as well."

Simon picked up his sword. "I must go. My help is needed on the field."

"The Maccabees are winning, aren't they?" asked Devorah.

Simon stopped. "Unfortunately, we're not doing well. There are too many enemy soldiers!"

"Wait!" Benjamin jumped up. "I know what you can do!"

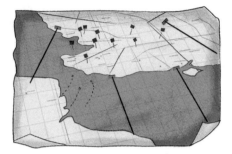

CHAPTER 8
GEORGE WASHINGTON

Everyone stared at Benjamin. "We've been studying about the American Revolution in school. George Washington's army was badly outnumbered, but he created many successful battle plans and he won the war."

"American Revolution? George Washington? More of your stories!! Who was this man you speak of?" asked Simon. "Was he a king?"

"No, he was . . . he was a great warrior fighting for freedom, just like the Maccabees," Devorah said.

"How do you know this?" asked Simon. "Did your parents fight in this great battle or is this more of your magic?"

Benjamin laughed. "Our parents? No, that war happened a long time ago . . . I mean . . ." He stopped and looked at his sister.

Devorah tried to explain. "The American Revolution happened centuries before we were born. We learned about it in school . . . the teachers tell us about what happened in history."

"I get it," said Shoshana. "Our rabbi and our parents pass along the traditions and laws from the Torah. Where you come from, your rabbis do the same thing, right?"

Devorah nodded.

"Tell me more about these battle plans!" insisted Simon.

"I'll tell you what I remember," said Benjamin. "General Washington convinced the British army, his enemy, that the American soldiers were unorganized and exhausted. Then he tricked the British by having the American soldiers leave the camp and hide. Washington left fire rings burning, as if his troops were still there. He even put up stuffed clothes to look like people."

Simon interrupted and asked, "What purpose was there in abandoning the camp?"

Benjamin continued. "The enemy, thinking it would be an easy victory, sent only a few of their troops to fight Washington's men. The others stayed in their camp, resting. Washington swooped down with his army on the small group of soldiers, surprising them because they thought the camp was empty, and easily defeated them. Then Washington attacked the enemy command center where the remaining soldiers were resting."

Simon shook his head. "This leader, Washington, took a big chance. The soldiers could easily have defeated his small army. I don't think Judah would take such a risk."

"It doesn't matter what *we* think," said Shoshana. She turned to Benjamin. "You must tell Judah what you know. Let him decide if this plan can work for the Maccabees."

"He won't be pleased to see you two again. But I'll take you to him." Simon motioned them to follow him.

The four children walked to the center of the camp. They found Judah pacing by the main campfire, hands clenched behind his back. He was arguing with another soldier. Devorah recognized the second man. It was Judah's brother, Jonathan. What would these men think when they saw her and Benjamin again?

Judah drew his sword. "What magic has allowed you to keep your youth over these last two years? If you are not spies, then you are surely demons or sorcerers."

"Judah," said Shoshana, in defense of her friends. "It doesn't matter how old they are. What's important is that we're struggling against a powerful enemy, and Benjamin has an idea that could help us win this war."

"I will not be guided by the words of a child," said Judah. "Especially a bewitched one!"

Jonathan interrupted. "Maybe we should listen to what he says, and then decide."

Judah pursed his lips and nodded. "It is only because of my concern for the fate of my people that I agree to hear this plan."

Benjamin described General Washington's strategy.

Judah smiled and nodded. "It might work," he whispered under his breath. He scowled at Benjamin. "Since we have no other option, we will try this plan of your Commander Washington. But for your sake, it had better prove successful!"

Benjamin turned to his sister as they all headed toward the main tent. "I just remembered something," he said with a grin.

"What?" asked Devorah.

"George Washington got the idea for his plans . . . from reading about the Maccabees!"

CHAPTER 9
BACK TO MODI'IN

Benjamin went with Jonathan and Simon to the main tent. The people had already assembled for the evening meal. As Simon explained the plan, Benjamin stuffed an old tunic with leaves and sat it on the ground. Placing the shirtsleeves over the open neck, the decoy appeared to be a man bending over. An excited murmur swept through the camp. This simple deception might give them the edge they needed to turn the war in their favor.

After a quick meal, the preparations began. The women and children gathered spare clothing and stuffed them with leaves while the Maccabees sharpened their swords. They packed dried meat, water pouches, and smaller weapons, supplies they would need for the upcoming battle. They worked through the night, resting only when the sun rose.

Just before dawn, Benjamin followed Simon and Jonathan as the men left camp and slipped back into Modi'in.

"We'll find our friends Luke and Samuel," Simon whispered to Jonathan. "They will help us with this part of the plan."

The friends agreed to help. Simon and Jonathan kept out of sight, as did Benjamin. They listened as Luke and Samuel strolled through the streets of Modi'in, stopping each time they passed a soldier.

"Luke, have you heard? The Jewish outcasts are losing their struggle with Antiochus' soldiers," said Samuel. The nearby soldier turned in their direction.

"Yes, I hear they are starving out there in the hills," replied Luke. "The people are exhausted. There is much sickness among the young and the elderly."

The men continued walking, pausing near a small group of guards gathered by the town's main well. Pulling up the bucket to get a drink, they continued chatting.

"Samuel, the Maccabees are fighting among themselves now. Some of the men are rebelling. Many want to return to the safety of Modi'in. Some are even refusing to fight."

"The camp is in chaos. It is lucky for them Antiochus' soldiers do not know the true situation. The Maccabees' struggle would be ended by even the smallest attack."

Simon and Jonathan watched long enough to see several soldiers gather. Benjamin held his breath as an argument broke out between them.

"If we attack the Maccabees now, we will defeat them once and for all," declared one guard.

"They are like scorpions, hiding everywhere and stinging whenever we come near. We should leave them alone until they run out of food. Then they will have to come to us!" A second guard shook his fist in the air.

"We must get this information to our commander. He will decide if it is time to attack the Maccabees!" shouted the first guard. He ordered a nearby soldier to return to the commander and tell him what they had overheard.

"Yes!" whispered Benjamin. "It worked!" He followed behind Jonathan and Simon as they headed back to camp.

The Maccabees had been working hard while the boys were gone. The stuffed figures were in place around the blazing campfire. The men and boys hid in nearby bushes, ready to attack. The women and children hid in nearby caves. Benjamin, Devorah, and Shoshana squeezed into a tiny cave a short distance from the camp. Afraid to speak, the children stared into the dark night. The silence was overwhelming.

Benjamin's legs twitched restlessly. "What if the plan doesn't work?" he whispered to his sister.

"This plan will work," Devorah assured him.

"If it doesn't," Benjamin said, "what will happen to George Washington? Will he lose to the British? It will be my fault if he loses!" He stood up and headed out of the cave. "I'm going back."

"What?" Devorah looked at her brother. "Are you crazy?"

"I've got to see if my plan is working. I can't just sit here and wait."

CHAPTER 10
CAPTURED

Shoshana grabbed Benjamin's arm. "Wait! What if someone sees you?"

Benjamin pulled free and raced out. The girls ran after him. Suddenly, shouting erupted all around them. They froze, eyes wide in terror, as enemy soldiers stormed the empty camp, swords drawn, slashing viciously through the air. Then, just as quickly, the soldiers stopped.

Angry voices filled the air.

"What is this?"

"The camp is empty. Where are they?"

"We have been deceived!"

"You two." The lead soldier singled out two guards. "Hurry back to our camp and tell the commander what has happened. The rest of you, spread out and search for the Maccabees. They must be nearby! They can't have gone far."

"Now!" Suddenly, the Maccabees rose from their hiding places and attacked the soldiers. The children could hear the fierce fighting and ran to the safety of their hiding place.

"Grab those children. We can use them as hostages!" shouted one of the two enemy soldiers.

Benjamin ran toward the soldiers, veering off at the last moment, drawing the men away from the girls.

"Catch him!" The two messenger soldiers turned and chased after Benjamin. He zig-zagged through the brush but couldn't evade them. His heart pounded as one of the guards jumped into the path in front of him.

Benjamin pivoted and ran to the right, but the second guard was there waiting for him. He tried to dodge around him, but the man grabbed his arm, lifting him into the air.

"Let me go!" shouted Benjamin.

"What do we have here?" asked the guard holding the struggling boy.

"A spy, following us to discover the location of our camp," said his companion.

Benjamin kicked his captor in the shin. The guard threw him to the ground and tied his hands behind his back. Benjamin prayed Devorah and Shoshana would stay hidden. He knew they were close enough to hear what was going on.

"What should we do with him?" the guard asked, rubbing his shin. "We must hurry. He will only slow us down."

As the soldiers discussed her brother's fate, Devorah searched the ground for a rock to use as a weapon to help him. Her hand closed on something. She put it in her pocket.

The guards approached Benjamin with their long, sharp swords drawn.

"Wait!" cried Benjamin. "Take me to your commander and I'll tell him what secrets I know."

The guards looked at one another. "Ignorant child—he knows nothing! He's not worth the trouble of keeping alive."

"It is not for us to decide. If our commander disagrees with you, we will be killed as well."

"And if the boy knows nothing?"

"Then I will kill him myself!"

The guards sheathed their swords, grabbed Benjamin, and headed back toward Modi'in.

The girls followed his trail. Devorah knew they could only help him escape if they stayed out of sight and didn't get captured as well.

CHAPTER 11
THE PLAN

Devorah worried that she and Shoshana would have a hard time following Benjamin. If the girls lost track of the guards, they'd never find her brother. She was relieved when she heard his voice. He kept talking to the guards as they traveled, making it easier for the girls to follow.

When they reached the camp, the soldiers dragged Benjamin to a large wooden enclosure tied to an outside gatepost. The guard watching the gate turned his back, ignoring Benjamin.

"Humph," mumbled the guard. "Now I'm a babysitter!"

A low whistle escaped Benjamin's lips as he glanced around. Through the bushes, the girls could see into the log enclosure behind him, where a herd of elephants moved restlessly.

The color drained from Shoshana's face. "What monsters are those?" she whispered.

"Elephants!" Devorah whispered back. She knew from the Hanukkah story that elephants were used in the battle of the Maccabees. *Ridiculous*, she'd thought when her teacher read the story. But there was nothing ridiculous about the huge animals, not to mention their awful stench. She could smell them from where she was hiding. Shoshana wrinkled her nose too at the strong smell. These animals were as fearsome as army tanks. Devorah was glad her brother was on the outside of the fence.

The girls circled the camp, careful to stay hidden. There were soldiers everywhere! Hundreds of them, and piles of weapons. Long silver swords, shorter daggers and axes, even a few scythes all sparkled in the midday sun. The Maccabees wouldn't stand a chance attacking this well-armed camp. Someone had to warn Judah to hold off on the second half of the plan. The Maccabees weren't prepared to battle this fortified camp.

"Shalom," said Benjamin in a raised voice.

Devorah and Shoshana returned to the bushes near the elephant enclosure.

The guard turned to Benjamin. "Are you speaking to me?"

"Yes. I don't like it here and I'd like to leave," he said.

Devorah could hear his voice shake. He talked bravely, but she knew he was scared.

"I'm sure you would," growled the guard. "Then you could warn your friends—tell them where we are. But do not worry. We will soon put you out of your misery . . . for good!"

When the guard looked the other way, Devorah saw her brother turn toward the bushes. *He must be looking to see if I'm here*, she thought. She waved the bottom of her white dress, hoping Benjamin could see it. He managed to give her a wobbly smile, then continued talking to the guard.

"Oh, I wouldn't tell the Maccabees where you are. I'd warn them to stay away. I'd tell them that you have way too many men, too many weapons . . . you even have elephants. No one could win against this heavily guarded, unbelievably strong camp." Benjamin's voice rose. "I would run and tell the Maccabees they should not plan to attack!"

"Your brother is telling us to return and warn Judah," whispered Shoshana. "The Maccabees can't

win in an attack on this camp! That part of Benjamin's plan won't work." She took Devorah's hand. "We must leave right away."

"You can go," Devorah pulled her hand away. "I'm not leaving my brother. I'm going to rescue him."

"Don't be foolish. You'll get yourself captured as well."

"I'm not going with you, but I have a plan." She whispered her idea to Shoshana. "You go and tell Judah. The Maccabees must be ready by the time my brother and I get there."

Shoshana shook her head. "Your plan has many things that could go wrong. But for it to work, you will need this." She handed Devorah a hunting knife. "May God be with you!" she said as she slipped away to warn the Maccabees.

Devorah stared at the camp, the guards, the huge elephants so close to her brother. Fear made her whole body shake. She clutched the knife, hoping she had the strength to carry out her plan. But she was determined. She would save her brother.

CHAPTER 12
SHOSHANA'S WARNING

When Shoshana arrived back at the Maccabees' camp, she froze. All around were tattered tents and broken cooking pots. Injured men lay everywhere, evidence of the fierce battle that had taken place.

Simon ran to her. "Shoshana! Blessed is God—you're okay! When I didn't see you return to camp after the battle, I was afraid you'd been captured by the soldiers . . . or worse."

Shoshana, panting from her desperate run, stared wide-eyed at her brother. Simon stopped talking. For the first time, he noticed the scratches on his sister's face and arms.

"Where are Devorah and Benjamin?" he asked. He reached up and untangled a bramble from her hair. "Did they try to steal you away with that cursed spinning top?"

Shoshana struggled to explain. "Benjamin got caught . . . swords . . . enemy camp. Stop! Stop the Maccabees!" Shoshana took a deep breath. "We have to stop Judah!"

"But the boy's plan has worked so far. We attacked the enemy soldiers in our camp as they tried to figure out where everyone was. We have captured or killed every enemy soldier. It's time to complete the second half of our plan by attacking the enemy camp."

"NO!" shouted his sister. "You can't fight at their camp. You won't win! They have too many men, weapons, even huge beasts called elephants!"

The fear in her voice shocked Simon. He grabbed his sister's hand and led her to Judah. She described the enemy's camp, the stacks of weapons, the elephants, the soldiers . . .

Judah's eyes flashed. "What have you done?" Shoshana cowered at his booming voice. "Spies! The newcomers are spies, just as I had first judged them to be! They will lead the enemy right to our camp!"

For the first time, Simon spoke up to defend Devorah and Benjamin. "It seems, Judah, that our strange friends have done us a great service. They have indeed acted as spies . . . spies for us! Now we know where our enemy's camp is and how strong a fighting force they have. We must prepare a new plan and defeat those soldiers."

Judah continued to glare, but his voice softened as Simon's words sank in. "Where are your friends?" he asked Shoshana.

"Devorah is hiding, watching the camp. But Benjamin . . ." Shoshana's voice dropped to a whisper. "Benjamin is a prisoner, tied up near the elephants. Two soldiers left our camp before the battle here had started. Benjamin drew them away from our hiding place. He was captured trying to protect us. But the soldiers reported to their commander that our site was deserted. They will try to force Benjamin to tell them our attack plans, and then they will kill him." The strain was too much. Tears flowed down her face.

"We need a new strategy. I see we lack the might to defeat the soldiers in their own camp." Judah stroked his beard. "We have to stall the soldiers, create a diversion of some type. We need to gain more time and a new plan before the soldiers return in strength."

Shoshana wiped away her tears and took a deep

breath. "Devorah had an idea for how to free her brother by creating chaos in the enemy's camp. Then she and Benjamin will lead the soldiers back here and into an ambush."

"Those are brave plans for a young girl," said Judah. "I am not convinced she can do it. Where will this ambush you speak of take place?"

Shoshana continued. "The soldiers brought Benjamin to their camp by following a path through a deep, narrow canyon. I returned here the same way. It is a good place for an ambush."

"How do we know the soldiers will come through the canyon?" Judah asked.

Shoshana shared the rest of Devorah's plan with Judah.

"I know this canyon, Judah. It will make an excellent site to attack our enemy." Simon put his hand on the hilt of his sword. "I can lead the attack!"

"You are a brave young man." Judah smiled. "But I need you for a more important task."

Simon couldn't hide his disappointment.

Judah pointed to Simon. "You and your sister must help the older children create slingshots. Tell each to gather a full pouch of stones."

Simon and Shoshana gathered the older children.

Simon held up a slingshot to demonstrate. "You put your stone in the band. Then pull back as hard as you can. Look directly at one of the huge beasts that will be carrying soldiers. Open your hand and the stone will fly to the beast and hit it. Their skin is thick, so it will not hurt them, but it will surprise them. Are you ready?" he asked, raising his slingshot.

The children raised their slingshots. "Ready!" they cried.

"What about us?" asked the youngest children.

"You will come with me," said Shoshana. "We'll hide in the caves here in the camp. We'll watch, and if any soldiers comes here, we will warn the Maccabees." She headed to the caves, where the young ones would be safe.

"Grab your weapons, men, and follow me!" shouted Judah. The Maccabees grabbed their swords and knives and hurried toward the canyon as Simon helped the older children up to their slingshot positions. Everyone waited. It was up to Devorah and her brother now.

CHAPTER 13
ESCAPE

Back at the enemy camp, Devorah also waited. She watched the guard from her hiding place, hoping for a chance to free her brother. A soldier came over and whispered something to the guard. Devorah couldn't hear them, but both men left, heading toward the center of the compound.

Devorah hurried around the elephant enclosure. She passed a second, larger gate. *That must be how they get the elephants in and out of the corral*, she thought. She made her way to her brother. Using Shoshana's sharp knife, she cut through his ties.

Devorah pointed to the other side of the enclosure. "There's a large gate in the back. Go open it," she instructed. "I'll cut the elephants loose."

Devorah knelt next to the largest elephant. Its huge

front left foot was tethered to the ground by strong ropes. The beast turned and stared right into her eyes.

"Oh, no!" Devorah gasped, leaping to her feet, ready to grab her brother and run. But the elephant turned its head away and rubbed its long trunk against the log fence. Devorah eased closer to its enormous foot and sawed through the thick rope. By the time she finished, her hands ached . . . and there were still more large beasts to free.

How am I ever going to finish? she thought. Thankfully, not all of the elephants were tethered, and she managed to slice the remaining bindings of those who were. The task seemed to take forever. She kept her eye on the camp, hoping the guards wouldn't return. As soon as she was done, she joined her brother by the back gate. They needed to find an elephant they could ride for the next part of her plan. A small elephant stood near the open gate. That one would have to work.

Devorah climbed up the log wall. She reached down to help her brother climb up to her. "I'll get on the elephant's back first and pull you up."

Benjamin was standing on the wall, clinging to the post, when the guard spotted them.

"The children are escaping!" he yelled.

Devorah shoved Benjamin onto the elephant's back. "Grab the hair on its head!" she yelled, scrambling up behind him. "Hold on tight!"

Kicking the elephant hard behind the ears, Devorah guided it further into the enclosure.

"You're going the wrong way!" shouted Benjamin to Devorah.

"We have to lead the elephants out—everything depends on that!" she cried.

With loud whoops and hollers, they chased the remaining beasts from the corral and scattered them into the camp. The soldiers scrambled out of the way of the huge feet. Tents crumbled, and food and supplies flew into the air as the elephants thundered by.

"What's going on? How did the elephants get loose?" shouted the commander.

"There!" the guard pointed to the small elephant. "It is the boy, and a second child as well. They must have released the elephants!"

"After them!" demanded the commander. "Do not let them escape!" He seized his spear and hurled it toward the children.

"Duck!" screamed Benjamin.

The spear whizzed by, just missing Devorah's ear.

"Let's get out of here!" she shrieked.

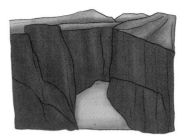

CHAPTER 14
THE CANYON

The children led their elephant away from the camp. The soldiers were running in all directions, trying to recapture the elephants. Devorah stopped urging their elephant forward.

"We can't get too far ahead," she told her brother. "The soldiers have to follow us into the canyon."

"Then can we get down for a while?" Benjamin shifted around on the elephant's back. "My tush hurts!"

Devorah sighed. "If we do that, we'll never be able to climb back up. I sure hope this elephant doesn't decide to wander back toward the camp."

The young elephant stopped at a bush filled with fat berries. It plucked the berries with its trunk and placed them into its mouth. Thankfully, the bush entertained the young elephant for a while.

"Listen," Devorah said suddenly. "It's quieting down. They must have caught all the elephants." A chill ran down her spine as she heard the commander shout new orders to his men.

"Find those children and bring me their heads!"

"I see an elephant in the distance," called a soldier. "It must be them!"

The soldiers headed toward them. Devorah guided the elephant back and forth, weaving a path through the trees. She led the soldiers toward the canyon, making sure to stay far enough away to be mostly out of sight. Devorah prayed that Shoshana had convinced Judah to use her new plan. What if Judah didn't like the plan and the Maccabees weren't at the canyon when the soldiers arrived? She couldn't bear to think about it.

The children stayed hidden in the trees, waiting for the soldiers to come a little closer.

"Where did they go?" asked one soldier.

"This path leads to the canyon," replied another. "They must be returning to their camp."

"Perfect!" whispered Devorah. "The plan is working."

"Halt!" said the commander. "I know a shorter way to the enemy camp. We will arrive at the same time as the children. Then we can capture them along with everyone else."

The soldiers turned away.

"No!" cried Devorah. "They're supposed to chase after us. They have to go through the canyon or the plan will fail!"

"What are we going to do?" asked Benjamin desperately.

"I don't know!"

Benjamin stood up on the elephant's back and yelled to the soldiers. "Hey, you stupid jerks!" The little elephant moved, startled by its rider's sudden explosion of noise. Benjamin wobbled and started to fall. Devorah grabbed his arm.

"What are you doing?" she whispered angrily at him. "You'll attract the soldiers' attention. They'll come after us!"

"Of course they will. That's the whole idea, isn't it?"

Devorah's eyes lit up with understanding. Grabbing onto the elephant's wrinkled skin, she started yelling as well. The soldiers spotted the children.

"There they are! The spies who released our elephants!"

"Catch them!"

The soldiers turned and chased after the children. But Benjamin and Devorah had a head start. They arrived at the canyon well ahead of the soldiers, but their elephant slowed when he reached the unfamiliar canyon path. The soldiers were catching up.

"Go faster, elephant!" cried Benjamin.

As the soldiers entered the narrow canyon, they were forced to reduce their speed. The commander, riding the lead elephant, hurled his spear. It soared past the children, glanced off a nearby rock, and bounced harmlessly in front of them. It was enough of a surprise, however, to startle the elephant. It reared in panic. The children held on tightly, but it was no use. They slid from its back, landing on the ground, and the elephant raced on without them.

Unable to see through the swirling dust, the children crawled toward the canyon wall and clung to each other as the thundering herd of their enemy's elephants drew near.

CHAPTER 15
THE AMBUSH

The leading elephants bellowed and stopped suddenly, sending soldiers flying over their heads.

Devorah could hear the pinging of small rocks. Elephants lumbered around in confusion as the rocks rained down on them from the steep canyon walls. Devorah squinted through the dust. Small figures dotted the walls . . . the Maccabees were fighting back!

The soldiers sought cover from the pelting rocks while trying to avoid the stampeding elephants. The air filled with angry shouts and loud trumpeting. Spears flew through the air, but this time they came from the other end of the canyon. The Maccabees marched toward the soldiers. Many of the soldiers fled through the canyon back toward their camp.

"Cowards!" cried their commander. "Stand and fight!"

"Not today," shouted a soldier as he passed. "These Maccabees fight with a mighty power helping them. We cannot fight their God."

The commander shook with anger. He turned and saw Devorah and her brother huddled against the canyon wall. He raised his spear, an evil smile on his face. "At least I will have one victory this day!"

"Devorah, do something!" screamed her brother.

"The dreidel!" Devorah suddenly remembered, reaching into her pocket. Her hand closed on the small top, which she had found and placed in her pocket when Benjamin was captured.

The commander threw his spear, but it clattered harmlessly against the rocks.

Devroah quickly knelt and spun the dreidel. Everything whirled around Devorah and Benjamin, whisking the children out of danger. The top spun faster and faster, then slowed, and stopped—just like that.

The Hebrew letter, *Hey*, was face up.

CHAPTER 16
HEY

Devorah feared the commander would still be there when she opened her eyes. But, finally, she peeked at the dreidel and saw the *Hey*—half good. In the dreidel game, the letter hey meant getting half the treasure . . . but here?

She glanced up, relieved to see they were no longer in the canyon. But they weren't at home either.

A frown spread across Benjamin's face. "Where are we this time?" He reached for the dreidel, but, as before, it had disappeared.

"*When* are we, you mean," replied his sister. She jumped up to join a group of Maccabees with their families heading down a dirt path. Everyone was laughing and singing.

"Look, it's Simon!" shouted Benjamin, as he

caught up to Devorah.

"Devorah! Benjamin!" Shoshana hurried over. "It's so good to see you again!"

Simon looked surprised to see them. "I thought you'd been trampled by the elephants."

Shoshana rolled her eyes at her brother. "Never mind him. Devorah, wait until you hear what's happened!"

"How long have we been gone?" asked Devorah.

"A little over a year. But listen. We've won! Benjamin, your plan to lure the enemy soldiers to our camp was a big success, the first of many victories. Antiochus' soldiers have left."

"We're returning to Jerusalem, to celebrate in the Temple!" said Simon.

"That's where we're heading now!" Shoshana danced as she walked.

"This is so great!" Benjamin said. "They won! We won! Everything will be okay now."

Devorah smiled. She couldn't wait to get to the Temple. She'd seen pictures of the magnificent Temple built so long ago in Jerusalem. And now she'd not only get to see it, she could go inside!

But as they drew near to the Temple, Devorah could see something was wrong. Simon and

Shoshana broke into a run. The children caught up to their friends inside the Temple.

"Oh, my!" whispered Devorah. She stepped around a pile of broken pottery. Shards of what used to be wine goblets, water jugs, and oil jars were everywhere.

"Devorah, look." Benjamin pointed to a huge pig wandering near what looked like the remains of an altar. Chickens pecked through weeds growing between the shattered tiles on the floor.

Someone nearby picked up a statue and smashed it angrily on the ground. "No idols in our Temple!" he cried, tears streaming down his face.

Everyone walked around in stunned silence. They picked through the rubble, searching for anything they could save. Fighting back tears, Devorah and her brother joined the Maccabees as they gathered the few remaining unbroken items.

Then they set to work cleaning up the Temple. It was a big job and took many days. The Maccabees scrubbed filth from the walls, replaced stone tiles, and rebuilt the ceremonial altar. When the altar was finished, everyone stopped to watch as the Temple priests came forward carrying a menorah, its seven gold branches gleaming in the fading sunlight. The elders had removed it from the Temple and hidden it before

the enemy soldiers came.

"The menorah was saved!" cheered the Maccabees.

As the menorah was placed above the door near the altar, Judah led the group in a prayer. "Blessed are You, Lord our God, Ruler of the Universe, who has given us life, sustained us, and allowed us to reach this day."

"I know that prayer!" Devorah sang along with the Maccabees. "We say it whenever something special happens," she whispered to Shoshana.

Slowly all traces of Antiochus' plundering were removed. The Temple stood clean but bare. Much had been stolen or destroyed by the soldiers. The people replaced missing items with their own cherished treasures—a pair of silver oil lamps for the Sabbath from one family, a hand-embroidered quilt to cover the Torah scrolls from another.

"We are ready to rededicate our Temple." Judah smiled. "Let us have the consecrated oil to light our menorah."

A murmur rumbled among the people. When they sorted through the damaged pottery, nobody had found a jar of oil. The rededication would have to wait.

CHAPTER 17
THE MIRACLE OF HANUKKAH

"Search the piles of shards behind the Temple. Try to find an unbroken jar of oil for the menorah," said Judah. "If we do not find any, we must wait to rededicate the Temple until new oil can be prepared and consecrated."

Devorah knew from her Sunday school studies that the holy oil Judah needed would take many days to prepare. She also knew, from the story of Hanukkah, that someone would find one small jar of oil. Maybe she could be the one! She hurried outside to search a pile of broken pottery off to the side of the Temple.

One by one the people re-entered the Temple shaking their heads. Benjamin returned, holding a small broken fragment from an oil jar. Devorah was the last to return. While searching through a small pile of fragments, she had found an unbroken jar of oil! Cradling it, she walked slowly into the Temple.

Devorah lifted up the jar. "I found some," she whispered.

Judah took the jar from her and raised it high in the air. "We have our oil!"

Devorah, smiling, backed up into the cheering crowd. Then she hurried to her brother and pulled him aside.

"Benjamin," she said softly. "Let's go."

"What do you mean, let's go?"

Devorah opened a small cloth she was holding. The jar of oil was not the only thing she had found in the rubble.

"The dreidel! You've found Bubbe's dreidel!" But the smile that spread across Benjamin's face was quickly replaced with a frown.

"We can't go now! We'll miss the celebration! And besides, you didn't find enough oil. That tiny jar won't last more than one night. We have to help them find more oil."

"They have enough oil. Don't you remember the Hanukkah story? The little jar of oil lasted eight days! That's the miracle of Hanukkah. Everything will be fine. This is their celebration, Benjamin. Let's go home and have ours."

Benjamin agreed. With the celebration going on behind them, the children sat down on the ground. Placing their hands on the dreidel, they gave it a slow spin. They let go and the top spun faster and faster. The Temple whirled with it, around and around. The children watched dizzily until the dreidel slowed its frantic dance and stopped—just like that. The golden *Gimmel* was face up.

Gimmel means you get everything!

CHAPTER 18
HOME AT LAST

The children looked around them and smiled. They were back home, back in their normal clothes, back in their living room. Jumping up, they raced to hug their parents.

"It's so good to be home!" Benjamin shouted.

"We've been gone so long!" Devorah grabbed her brother's hands and danced in a circle.

"Gone? What are you talking about?" Zayde asked. "You've been right here the whole time. Look."

Devorah, ready to argue, looked to where Zayde was pointing. Her argument froze in her mouth. The night's eight Hanukkah candles still glowed brightly in the hanukkiah.

Benjamin stared. "But that's not possible. We went back in time. We spent months fighting and hiding."

"It took forever just to clean the Temple!" Devorah looked at her brother. "Did we dream it all?"

"Look at the candles," Bubbe pointed out with a shrug. "Nothing has changed."

"No, Bubbe," said Benjamin. "Everything has changed. I helped the Maccabees win the war against Antiochus!"

"And I found the oil for them!" said Devorah.

"And I found . . ." Benjamin opened his hand, revealing a small fragment of pottery. "I found this."

Devorah smiled at her brother. It wasn't a dream.

Mom took Bubbe's dreidel, packed it carefully in its golden box, and took it upstairs.

"What are you going to do with it, Mom?" Benjamin asked.

"I'm putting it away for now."

"For now?" Benjamin asked.

"Yes, it will be here, safe and sound, until you need it . . ." Mom patted the box and smiled, ". . . for your own children."

"Are you ready for your presents now?" asked Bubbe.

"Our presents?" Devorah looked at the gifts piled on the fireplace hearth.

Benjamin picked up a box with his name on it. "I guess so."

Dad winked at Mom. "They don't seem as eager to open their presents."

"I keep thinking about our . . . our dream." Devorah took the small box Mom held out to her. "Everyone brought gifts to the Temple after Antiochus's soldiers ruined it. It almost seems weird to be getting a present instead of giving one."

Benjamin set his present down. "I know! Let's give everyone else their gifts first, Devorah." He raced into his bedroom and returned with four paintings.

"You and Dad love cars," he said, handing two paintings to Dad and Zayde.

"This is beautiful!" Mom exclaimed, holding up her painting of a vase of flowers.

Bubbe's eyes were filled with tears. Her painting was a Shabbat dinner table, complete with their family gathered around two glowing candles.

"And I made your favorite animals out of clay," said Devorah, returning from her bedroom with four small boxes. There was a panda for Bubbe, a tiger for Zayde, a long-necked giraffe for Mom, and a lion for Dad.

"How about opening *your* gifts now?" Mom asked.

"Let's eat our latkes first," suggested Benjamin. "I'm sure Bubbe and Zayde are hungry after their long car ride to get here."

"That way we can watch the candles and remember the miracle of Hanukkah," added Devorah.

The two children gazed at the flickering lights, reflecting on all they had seen during their journey to Modi'in. The flames burned as brightly as hope and determination had burned in the hearts of the courageous friends they had met and would never forget.

THE END